Dedicated to my two beautiful sons,
Drake and Logan, who inspired me to
write this story, and to my husband,
Derek, who has given me unending love
and support.

-Brittany Jo Jones

Drake the Dragon King

Copyright © 2013 by Brittany Jo Jones

All rights reserved. No part of this publication may be reproduced or transmitted in any form or by any means, electronic or mechanical, including photocopy, recording, or any information storage and retrieval system, without permission in writing from the publisher.

Requests for permission to make copies of any part of the work should be submitted online at info@mascotbooks.com or mailed to Mascot Books, 560 Herndon Parkway #120, Herndon, VA 20170.

PRT0813A

Library of Congress Control Number: 2013943769

Printed in the United States

ISBN-10: 162086360X
ISBN-13: 9781620863602

www.mascotbooks.com

DRAKE THE DRAGON KING

Brittany Jo Jones

Illustrated by
Kristopher Grimes, PhD

Once upon a magical time,
Across a land so vast with fields of vine,
Across rivers so large and seas so blue,
Sat a rocky old cove that had something due.

A fire flickered upon the rough, rocky walls,
As reflections of new life was called.

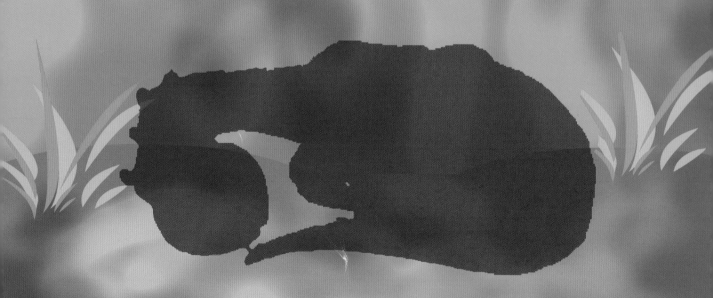

A baby dragon was born.

With wings of silver and scales of slate,
As lore would have it, this dragon was indeed fate.

They called him Drake, and he was handsome indeed.
He flew the skies so swift, so free.

He had many friends who admired him so.
He sat on top of the world, never below.
But one day, he knew something was wrong,
As his usual take off was not swift at all.

He ran so fast and flew off the ground,
When at last, at a halt, he tumbled down, down, down.
He pondered all day, he pondered all night.
He couldn't fathom what was wrong with his flight.

He went to his cove where he fell fast asleep,
But woke close to dawn, and leapt to his feet.
He felt a sharp twinge in his left silvery wing.

As he approached his mother, chanting,
"Mother, it stings!"
Mother Dragon gazed upon Drake's wing,
Then she remembered the story in the
Great Book of Kings.

She sat comfortably in her old little nook
And began telling the story from this ancient book.
As legend foretold, a dragon would come forth,
And rule the great lands that lie to the North.

Drake asked his mother, "Is this legend about me?"
"My dear little dragon, yes indeed."
Mother Dragon explained,
"In order for you to be king,
Something special must fall from your wing."

As Mother Dragon had a long hard gaze,
She was filled with joy and utterly amazed
At the golden gem that shined as bright as the
sun's rays.

It would take several months for the
gem to fall out,
But until that day came, Drake was
harshly talked about.

Kids would laugh and have a great fly,
As Drake sat sadly back and watched the
time pass by.
He was no longer admired, as kids thought
he was strange,

But his mother explained, "One day this will change.
You will be king and admired by all,
As you fly high in the skies and stand boldly tall."

"But until then, others can be mean and they
don't understand,
That the dragon they mock, will rule the land."

"So my dear little dragon, do not be sad.
Go out and about, be joyous, be glad."

Drake went out with his head held up,
Amongst all the chatter, amongst all the talk.

He did this for months until suddenly one day,
He looked to his wing and noticed the gem
was astray.

He looked to the ground and there it lay,
He picked it up and ran fast away.
He ran to the cove where the legend foresaw,
To show his mother what lay in his claw.

"My dear little dragon, the day has come.
Let's fly to the North and sound all the drums."

"For you are now king and will be admired by all,
The days of mockery made their last call.
You will rule the land and teach kindness and love,
For you, my little dragon, were sent from above."

Mother leaned up to kiss him, for now he was tall
And Drake no longer felt mocked, but rather
loved by all.

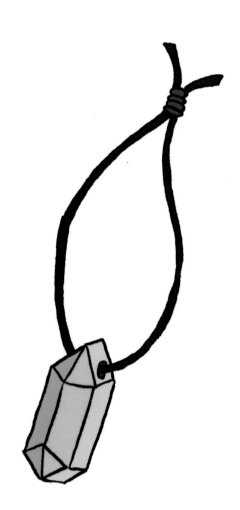

The End

About the Author

Brittany Jo Jones began exploring her love of writing from an early age by simply handwriting letters to relatives. Even when the internet and email became full circle, she still felt there was something so personal about writing with pen and paper. It wasn't until her senior year in high school, 2001, that she decided she wanted to be a professional writer.

In 2002, at the age of twenty, she moved with her United States Air Force husband across the world to Japan. In her spare time, she began writing poetry. By the time 2006 rolled around, she had a binder full of poetry, and Brittany and her husband were getting ready for their next adventure in the United Kingdom where her professional writing career took off. Being in the UK made her writing even more prominent because that is where some of her most beloved authors, Jane Austin in particular, resided. She's been published in magazines and newspapers for journalistic and creative pieces. In 2011, she began writing her first children's book, *Drake the Dragon King.*

While in the UK, Brittany had two sons, and it was her own children, with their wildly imaginative personalities, that inspired her to write stories for children. It was her family's love of mythical creatures, like dragons and elves, that gave her the idea to begin writing the story of Drake the Dragon.

J
JON

3.14

DATE DUE			
JUN 2 1 2014			
JUL 0 3 2014			
APR 2 1 2016			
OCT 0 4 2016			
OCT 2 8 2016			
MAR 2 4 2017			
JUN 0 9 2017			